Blood Buns
and Scarecrows

Written by Sheryl Webster

Illustrated by Pete Williamson

The Fang Family

Small Fang

Father Fang

Veino

Grandpa Fang

Mother Fang

Baby Fang

Did you know?

Vampires …
- can change into bats.
- have red eyes and fangs.
- often sleep in coffins.
- *hate* garlic.
- *love* to drink blood!

Funny Fang Family Fact:

Grandpa Fang's eyesight is so bad that he sometimes mistakes scarecrows for real people!

Let's Fly!

Father Fang was working late at the blood bank.

Mother Fang was putting Baby Fang to bed. "Sweet nightmares," she whispered as she laid Baby in her cotfin.

So there was only Small Fang who could go late-night shopping with Grandpa. Actually, Small Fang was looking forward to it. Shopping with Grandpa was NEVER dull!

Grandpa Fang grabbed his
shopping list from the fridge.

Blood buns
More blood buns
Extra blood buns —
in case of visitors!

Small Fang peered at it. "Oh Grandpa!" he giggled. "We keep telling you. They're not blood buns. They're jam doughnuts!"

7

Grandpa popped his false fangs into his mouth and changed into a bat. "Let's fly!" he cackled. "I'll race you!"

The journey was not easy – not
with Grandpa's poor eyesight. First,
Small Fang had to scoop him off
a tree.

Then he had to peel Grandpa
from three car windscreens and
two buses.

"The city is too busy," grumbled a very crumpled Grandpa. "Let's fly over the countryside."

As they flew over Farmer Pickles's field, Grandpa thought he spotted something tasty.

"You go on," he said slyly to
Small Fang. "I'll just rest for a bit."

Smelly Bat Breath

Small Fang hung around waiting for Grandpa outside the supermarket.

"Better late than never," chirped Grandpa Fang as he swooped down. "Let's get a trolley."

Inside the supermarket, Grandpa didn't see the girl carefully putting the last tin on the huge pile.

Crash!

"Sorry," apologised Small Fang. "Grandpa is as blind as a bat."

Nor did Grandpa see the baker carrying his tray of fresh cream cakes topped with red cherries.

"My beautiful cakes!" he cried.

"Whoops! Sorry ..." said Grandpa, "but they do taste much better topped with clotted blood. You should try it."

Whoops!

At the bakery counter, Grandpa
got out his list. "Twenty-five blood
buns, please," he said.

Small Fang smiled. "Erm ... sorry!
My Grandpa means jam doughnuts,"
he explained.

Grandpa was so excited that he
shoved two into his mouth at once.

Suddenly he began to cough …
and splutter … and choke! He tried
to chew, but he couldn't.

Small Fang patted him hard
on the back. Out flew the two
doughnuts. **Wheeeeeee**! They landed
with a splat on the baker's glasses.

"I don't know what happened," said Grandpa. "My false fangs wouldn't work!" He opened his mouth wide, filling the supermarket with his smelly bat-breath.

"They're not working because they're not there!" explained Small Fang. "You must have lost them."

They looked all over the supermarket, but could not find the fangs. Where could they be?

3
Grandpa's Revenge

"Maybe I dropped my fangs outside," dribbled Grandpa. "Let's pay for the blood buns, then look for my fangs on the way home."

However, just as they got to the checkout, a rude lady shoved her trolley in front of them. Grandpa frowned. Then he had an idea.

He lifted the bag of blood buns
from his trolley, changed into his
wings and flew in front of the rude
lady. Then he changed back.

The rude lady blinked, rubbed her eyes and fled out of the supermarket. Grandpa and Small Fang howled with laughter.

"I don't think she's a member of your fang club, Grandpa!" joked Small Fang.

Hide and Shriek

Grandpa and Small Fang decided to walk home and have some fun.

"Fangcy a game of Hide and Shriek?" asked Grandpa.

"Oh yes!" said Small Fang, grinning wickedly.

So Grandpa and Small Fang did the hiding, and passers-by did the shrieking!

Then, Grandpa and Small Fang chased after their victims.

"Sorry!" they shouted. "It was just a joke. Here, have a blood bun!"

But the sight of Grandpa, with jam gushing down his hands, just made them run faster.

Grandpa and Small Fang were tired after all that giggling, so they flew the rest of the way home.

When they got there, Grandpa was feeling hungry. It was only then that he remembered his lost fangs. Oh no! He had forgotten to look for them.

Just then the doorbell groaned. Grandpa opened the creaky door. There stood Farmer Pickles, looking angry. In one hand, he held his torn and tatty scarecrow. In his other hand, he held something else.

"I think these belong to you," he said. He handed Grandpa his lost fangs. "Now, will you please leave my scarecrow alone?"

Grandpa looked guiltily at Small Fang. "He just looked so delicious. And I was hungry on our way to the supermarket!"

Grandpa took his false fangs from Farmer Pickles and popped them in. "Thank you!" he said. "Now ... do you fancy staying for a bite?"